Silent Movie

Silent Movie

The Production Company

Avi . . . . The Author

C. B. Mordan . . . . . The Illustrator

The Cast of Characters

Papa....................................From Sweden, intrepid immigrant to America

Mama...His hard-working wife

Gustave...Their young son

A Thief..Even in America

A Friend from the Old Country.........The best friends are old friends

Bartholomew Bunting....................................Famous movie director

Atheneum Books for Young Readers

New York • London • Toronto • Sydney • Singapore

'For Anne Schwartz
—Avi

'For Avi, and the Ryan family
—C. 'B. 'M.

Atheneum Books for Young Readers
An imprint of Simon & Schuster Children's Publishing Division
1230 Avenue of the Americas
New York, New York 10020
Text copyright © 2003 by Avi
Illustrations copyright © 2003 by C. B. Mordan
Book design by Ann Bobco and Kristin Smith
The text of this book is set in Gararond.
The illustrations are rendered in ink on clayboard.
Manufactured in China

10 9 8 7 6
Library of Congress Cataloging-in-Publication Data
Avi, 1937-
Silent movie / Avi, the author : C. B. Mordan, the illustrator.—
1st ed.
p. cm.
Summary: In the early years of the twentieth century, a Swedish
family encounters separation and other hardships upon immigrating
to New York City until the son is cast in a silent movie.
ISBN 978-0-689-84145-3
[1. Immigrants—New York (N.Y.)—Fiction. 2. Emigration and
immigration—Fiction. 3. Silent films—Fiction.] I. Mordan, C. B.,
ill. II. Title.
PZ7.A953 Si 2002
[E]—dc21
2001033025
0814 SCP

One hundred years ago people from all over the world
are moving to the United States of America. Some want
adventure. Some are fleeing hardship. Others come because
they believe America is "The Promised Land."
Among those who seek a better life is a family
from Sweden. The first to go is Papa . . .

Six months later.
It's time for Mama and Gustave to join Papa.

Three days later.
Their money gone, the only way
to get food is by begging.

A little money at last.

A thief. He steals from the poor
to make himself rich.

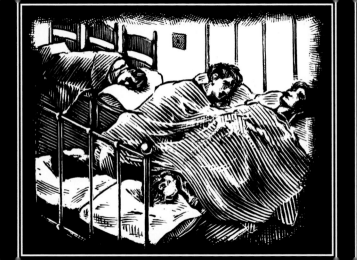

. . . and a job for Mama.
It pays one dollar a week.

Bartholomew Bunting,
famous movie director.

Movies are shown in nickelodeons. They are
all the rage, and only a nickel to see.

Bunting plans an action movie.
"We need a child actor."

"So what? Movies are silent. Tell his mother
I'll pay him a dollar a day."

Meanwhile sad Papa
is still looking for his family.

Weary, Papa takes a break . . .
at the nickelodeon.

On the screen he sees a familiar face.
"That's my boy!"

GUSTAVE IS **THE**
WONDER BOY
A BARTHOLOMEW BUNTING PRODUCTION

AUTHOR'S NOTE

Movies were invented in the late nineteenth century. They were usually very short in length, had black-and-white images, and, until "talkies" arrived in 1929, were silent. Acting was melodramatic. Stories were simple, and were interrupted by printed words—called titles—to explain parts of the plot or give bits of dialogue. Often a piano player (or organist) played dramatic music to help set the mood. Silent movies were popular in cities, particularly among immigrants because they were cheap—often just a nickel—and language was not a barrier.

When I was a child you could still see silent movies at special theaters. Charlie Chaplin, Laurel and Hardy, Buster Keaton were favorites of mine. When I saw some of C. B. Mordan's work, I was struck, not just by its dramatic impact, but by the way each image told a story—not unlike frames in a silent movie.

Like silent movies, picture books tell a story mostly through pictures, and with just a few words. In the best picture books, visual discovery comes frame-by-frame, leading to an eye-filling, heart-moving dramatic climax. And when a reader is alone, it can happen just as silently as an old movie. Best of all, both books and movies can be watched and enjoyed again and again.

ILLUSTRATOR'S NOTE

Doing research for this book was great fun—I watched lots of silent movies. I learned that the old movies, with so little written—and no spoken—information, relied almost exclusively on visual elements to tell the story. Characters were often set in stark contrast to one another, and revealed themselves through dramatic expressions. Some scenes were busy and brightly lit; others showed actors in extreme close-up, surrounded by darkness.

   The real challenge was figuring out how to interpret the experience of watching a silent movie in a picture-book format. How could I make action speed by for the audience, and contemplative moments pass more slowly? At last I hit upon a solution: to translate time into space on the page. And so I've created smaller images to show a quick sequence of events; most larger images are for stiller, more emotionally packed moments.

   I hope that when you look at *Silent Movie,* it will, at least in some part, feel like sitting in a darkened theater as another world opens up before you.

~The End~